BILLIE and BEAN in the CITY

Julia Hansson

Translated from Swedish
by B.J. Woodstein

ORCA BOOK PUBLISHERS

Mom has gone to do the laundry.
Billie is taking care of Bean.

Bean wants to go out now.

Billie went out with
Bean once before.
Mom watched
through the window.

They are just going to
go around the block.

Bean finds some
ice cream.

"What's your dog's
name?" a mother asks.
"Bean," says Billie.

Oh no! Bean is eating a flower.

The florist gives Billie a flower. "What a cute dog you have," she says.

DOG ROSES 20=
CATNIP 10=
SUNFLOWERS 30=
TIGER LILIES 50=
KITTENTAILS 10=

"No, Bean! We can't go to the park!"

Oh, Bean just
needed to poo.
Billie has a bag.

There are more flowers here. Billie can make a bouquet for Mom.

Oh no!
Billie doesn't
recognize
where she is.

Where are
Billie and Bean?

What if they never get back home?
Then Mom will be all alone.

Where is Bean going now?

They found their way home!

Now they need to rest.

"Mom!"

"You did a good job taking
care of Bean," says Mom.